OSCAR THE GROUCH!

Zoe

Cookie Monster

Count Von Count

THIS BOOK BELONGS TO:

Leo

From,
Chris and Kathryn

BERT

Snuffy

Prairie Dawn

Designed by Bendon Publishing International, Inc.

ISBN-13: 978-1-4351-4260-2

Manufactured in China
Lot #:
2 4 6 8 10 9 7 5 3 1
06/12

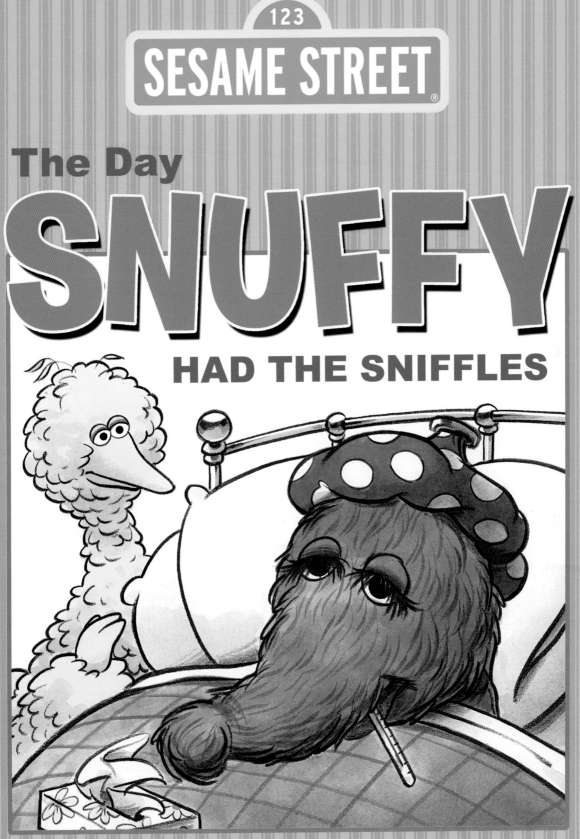

123 SESAME STREET®

The Day SNUFFY HAD THE SNIFFLES

by **Linda Lee Maifair**

illustrated by
Tom Brannon

Sandy Creek
NEW YORK

Oscar popped out of his can and saw Big Bird rushing down Sesame Street.

"Where are you going, Bird?" Oscar said. "It looks like you're in a hurry."

"I am," Big Bird said. "I'm going to Snuffy's house. He has the sniffles."

"Grouches know a lot about the sniffles," said Oscar.
"I have just the thing. Wait here!" Oscar disappeared into
his can.

Big Bird was waiting for Oscar when Cookie Monster came along.

"What's going on?" Cookie asked.
"Snuffy's got the sniffles," Big Bird said. "I'm waiting for Oscar. He has something for Snuffy."
"Me too!" said Cookie. "Wait here!"

When Bert heard that Snuffy had the sniffles,
he said, "I know just the thing to cheer up a sniffly
Snuffleupagus. Wait here!"

Bert came back and handed Big Bird a shoe box.
"It's my bottle-cap collection," Bert said proudly. "It
will give Snuffy something to look at while he's sick."

Huffing and puffing, Cookie Monster came back. He held out a dented cookie tin.

"Thanks, Cookie," Big Bird said. He tugged at the lid. "I just know Snuffy will enjoy all these... COOKIE CRUMBS?"

"Well, it's the thought that counts," said Cookie.

Finally, Oscar popped out of his can. "Here,
Bird," he said. "It's an old Grouch family recipe—
sardine-and-sauerkraut soup! It's sure to cure even
Snuffleupagus-sized sniffles," Oscar said.

"Don't let that soup get too warm." said Oscar.
"Sardine-and-sauerkraut soup only tastes its worst
when it's cold."

Juggling the shoe box, the cookie tin, and the smelly Grouch soup, Big Bird started off again. He got as far as the library when he met Betty Lou.

"I know just the thing to cheer up Snuffy," Betty Lou said.

"Here are some books for Snuffy to look at.
There's nothing like a good book to cheer you up!"
said Betty Lou.

"What do you have there, Big Bird?" the Count asked from his castle.

Big Bird told the Count he was bringing get well gifts to Snuffy. "I have just the thing," the Count said. "Wait there!"

The Count came out of his castle and handed
him a box of tissues.
"Snuffy can count them as much as he pleases,
and they'll come in handy whenever he sneezes!" the
Count said.

"My, my, you have your hands full," said Gladys the cow.

"These are for Snuffy," Big Bird explained. "He has the sniffles. I'm going to cheer him up."

"Well, there's only one way to do that," Gladys said. "Wait here!"

Gladys returned with a pint of ice cream.
"Nothing puts you in a good mooood like ice
cream," Gladys said.

At last Big Bird made it to Snuffy's cave without dropping a single present.

Then he had a terrible thought. "I brought all these presents for Snuffy and not a single one of them is from me! I hope he won't be disappointed," he said.

Snuffy was propped up in his Snuffleupagus-sized bed. Mrs. Snuffleupagus took the thermometer out of Snuffy's mouth. "No more fever!" she said.

Then, she took a bottle and measured orange sniffles medicine into a spoon. Snuffy swallowed it all. Mrs. Snuffleupagus gave him a big hug.

"Uh-oh!" Big Bird said. The presents were slipping from his grasp.
"Ah...Ah...CHOO!" Snuffy sneezed a gigantic snuffle sneeze. The presents crashed to the floor!
Big Bird stood in the doorway, feeling very sad.

Snuffy smiled at Big Bird. "Oh, Bird," he sniffled, "you brought the best gift to cheer me up."

Big Bird stared at the mess on the floor. "What's that, Snuffy?" he asked.

"A visit from you!" said Snuffy. That cheered up Big Bird, too!